Thanks a Lot!

by

Lucille R. Kraiman

Butte Publications, Inc.
Hillsboro, Oregon, U.S.A.

Thanks a Lot!

© 1995 Butte Publications, Inc.

Reviewers: Connie Knepper
                  Minnie Mae Wilding-Diaz
Editor: Ellen Todras
Cover: Anita Jones
Page Design: Anita Jones

Butte Publications, Inc.
P.O. Box 1328
Hillsboro, Oregon 97123-1328
U.S.A.

ISBN 1-884362-05-2
Printed in U.S.A.

To my kids: Mike, Dan and Ruth

Thanks a lot - for all your
encouragement!

Special thanks to Lew Keller and Connie Knepper for their invaluable information and help. Ongoing thanks to my cousin Charlotte and my publisher, Matt Brink.

Table of Contents

Chapter 1

Jordan stopped outside the fourth grade room. It was his first day in Clay Elementary School. Not a school for the deaf. And he was deaf.

He couldn't hear at all without his aids. He couldn't hear much with them. But he could read lips. And he could sign fast.

Would the kids here understand signing? He pushed back his blond hair and looked into the classroom. The smell of pencil shavings and clean paper drifted toward him. At least it smelled like his old classrooms.

Kids were walking around the room, talking to each other. School had started two days ago.

He rubbed the knuckles of his right hand. If only his dad hadn't changed jobs. And cities. Then he'd still be with signing friends, not with hearing kids. He bet these kids didn't sign at all.

His parents had visited the principal last week. They'd been told he'd have an interpreter.

But how could he make friends?

Jordan stared into the room. Fear dried his tongue. He didn't see any teacher or any interpreter.

What a mess! These kids wouldn't understand him. If he was lucky, there was another deaf kid in this class. Jordan felt a hand slap his shoulder. He whirled around.

A tall brown-skinned boy smiled and said something fast.

Jordan saw his lips move and heard voice sounds. He couldn't make out the words. He pointed to his hearing aids and signed, *Speak slow.*

The boy laughed. Then he leaned toward Jordan's aids and shouted.

Jordan jumped and back and shook his head. Loud sounds hurt his ears.

The boy didn't understand. He frowned and went into the room.

Jordan ground his teeth. That boy expected him to speak out loud. Well, he didn't. It was difficult to say words he couldn't hear clearly.

In his other school all the kids had been deaf and they used only sign language. They were proud to be deaf. So was Jordan.

A skinny boy sprinted across the room. He pushed two girls out of his way. He stopped in front of Jordan. His dirty-socks smell blocked the doorway.

Jordan saw the boy's mouth move. He could hear some sounds and he could read the boy's lips.

"Who are you?" the boy asked.

Without thinking, he signed. *My name is Jordan.*

The boy's eyebrows shot up. "A deafie!" he yelled. He waved his hands near Jordan's nose, making fun of Jordan's sign language.

Jordan stepped back. *I don't like this guy. He's a jerk. And he stinks!*

A pretty brown-eyed girl came toward the door. She frowned at the obnoxious boy waving his hands. She shook her long black hair. "Lea-ve him a-lo-ne, Ma-x," she said.

The boy opened his mouth wide. He yelled, "The other deafie!" Then he poked the girl's arm and dashed away.

This class was a big mistake, Jordan thought. *I want to go back to my deaf school.*

The girl stood in front of him. She wore a plastic strap around her neck. A small blue box hung from it.

"My na-me is Li-sa," she said. "I am dea-f too." She pointed to hearing aids in both her ears. She pointed to the plastic box. "FM," she said. "Ge-t from te-cha-."

I don't understand, Jordan signed. He waited for Lisa to sign something.

But she didn't. She shook her head vigorously. "I don't sign," she said. She walked away and sat down, facing the teacher's desk.

Jordan had wished for another deaf classmate and here she was. But she didn't speak his language!

Jordan noticed that the other boys and girls sat down. He saw a red light blinking on the wall. Maybe it was the signal for class to start.

Jordan walked to an empty desk at the front of the room.

Lisa watched him. The tall boy turned and stared.

3

Jordan swallowed hard, but a lump stayed in his throat. At his old school he made kids laugh. He was popular.

But here no one could understand him. How could he make them laugh? He didn't belong here. How would he understand the teacher? And...where was his interpreter?

Chapter 2

A short, red-haired man hurried into the room. He stopped in front of Jordan and faced him.

Jordan understood what he lipread.

Hello, signed the man. *Your interpreter is sick today. I am Mr. Allrite, your teacher. Welcome to class.*

Ha, thought Jordan. Mr. Allrite... Not all right I bet. But he really can sign. Jordan noticed a tiny microphone clipped on his teacher's shirt.

The teacher went to his desk and got something from a drawer. He brought it to Jordan. *For you*, he signed. *It's an FM. Have you ever used one before?* He held out a blue plastic box on a strap. It was just like the box the deaf girl wore.

Jordan put it over his head. Two thin wires with plugs dangled loose. *What now?* he signed.

Mr. Allrite went behind his desk. He signed, *Lisa can show you how the FM works.* He motioned to the pretty brown-eyed girl.

Lisa stood next to Jordan, waiting.

Mr. Allrite said something. Then he signed, *Can you hear me?*

Jordan shook his head.

The teacher touched the microphone. He pointed to Lisa. *Receiver on*, he signed and said.

She plugged the wires into Jordan's hearing aids. She flipped a switch on his blue box.

"Can you hear me now?"

Jordan lipread what Mr. Allrite asked. And he could hear him!

The teacher spoke to the class. Then he signed to Jordan. *I said you are new to our school. I want you feel welcome. The kids know you can't hear. They know you can use sign language, but don't speak. Your interpreter will be here tomorrow.*

Lisa has a different interpreter. I'll teach the kids to sign some words so they can talk with you. I have a deaf brother and sign a lot with him.

Mr. Allrite spoke to the class. Then he signed. "This is *Hello* or *Hi*. He moved his hands and fingers. "This is *okay*."

Lisa watched a young woman who sat facing her. That must be her interpreter, thought Jordan. I wonder when she came in?

He listened to Mr. Allrite's voice. He lipread the words that went with the sounds. It wasn't easy to do.

"Lisa." The teacher smiled and said something.

She shook her head energetically.

Jordan could hear some sounds. But he couldn't lipread without signs.

6

The teacher spoke to Lisa and signed. *I know you didn't learn sign, but I hope you will. Jordan, maybe you can learn to speak some words. Then all the kids could understand you better.*

Mr. Allrite put on a pair of horn-rimmed glasses and held up a thick, green book. He pointed at Lisa and said something.

She got up from her desk next to Jordan's. She brought him another green book. She sat down and faced her interpreter and the teacher.

Hey, she watches lips just like me, Jordan realized. I bet she can learn to sign. Then she would be a friend I could talk to. Jordan fidgeted in his seat. What if Lisa didn't <u>want</u> to learn his language? Then he'd have no friends at all!

The morning dragged by—math, then social studies. When Mr. Allrite gave instructions, he signed. He usually spoke out loud too.

Jordan watched the teacher's lips and face. He listened to the sounds. It was a new way for him to learn. So difficult. He wished his interpreter was here. He wished he was back with his signing friends.

The red wall light flashed again. Mr. Allrite spoke without signing. Jordan couldn't understand what he said.

The tall, brown-skinned boy came over and faced Jordan. As he spoke, Jordan read his lips. "The bell rang." The boy turned and pointed to the red light. Then he faced Jordan again. He motioned, *eating.*

Jordan noticed the clock. Of course. Lunchtime. But where should he go? He felt uncomfortable and frowned.

7

Mr. Allrite came over and stood in front of Jordan. *This is Abdul*, the teacher signed. *He'll take you to the cafeteria.*

Jordan followed Abdul out of the room and down the hall. He stuck his hands in his jeans pockets. His stomach rumbled in anticipation of lunch.

He wondered if they served hot dogs and burgers here. Those were his favorites—even pizza would be okay.

He bet the lunch workers didn't sign. No problem. He would point to the food he wanted and they would understand.

But there were no hot dogs, no burgers, no pizza. And there were problems!

The people dishing out food didn't understand him. Jordan pointed to the spaghetti. The woman filled a small spoon. She dumped a little bit of spaghetti and tomato sauce on his plate. Jordan signed, *I want more.* She shrugged, then dished Abdul.

Jordan pointed to the salad. Another woman filled a slotted spoon. The crisp carrot and radish shreds fell through. All he got was plain, wilted lettuce.

Now he came to the butterscotch pudding. He didn't like this at all, so he shook his head.

The serving man grinned and reached for a huge soup bowl. He poured in pudding and placed the bowl on Jordan's tray.

Abdul touched his shoulder, laughed, and said something.

Jordan shrugged and followed Abdul to a table. He hadn't heard him, but maybe they could be friends anyway.

Mr. Allrite came by. *Everything okay?* he signed.

8

Abdul and Jordan both grinned.

Jordan was so hungry, he ate most of the gooey pudding.

Abdul opened his mouth and his lips moved. "You ate all that slop."

Jordan lipread and laughed.

Abdul's lips moved again. Very fast. "Wanna......me?"

Jordan tried to lipread, but the words didn't make sense.

Abdul got up and started walking away.

Jordan grabbed his arm. He pointed to one hearing aid and to his mouth.

Abdul shouted in his ear. Jordan winced with the pain. He shook his head and held a finger over his mouth in "shh" position. Then he made Abdul stand still and turn to face him.

Abdul grinned. He spoke again—slower, without shouting. "Wanna... soccer with me?"

Jordan sighed. Communication with hearing kids was so difficult. But he understood enough and he could play soccer without talking.

That afternoon, Mr. Allrite reviewed the signs. *Hello.* He moved his hands and fingers. *Okay.* "Tomorrow I'll teach you how to tell your name. Class dismissed."

The teacher stopped Jordan. *How did it go today?* he signed.

Jordan frowned. What was he supposed to say. That everything was fine?

Well, it wasn't. He had to work so hard. And only this teacher really talked to him.

Mr. Allrite smiled. *Your interpreter will be here tomorrow*, he signed. *It will be easier for you.*

Yeah, sure, signed Jordan. He started

9

walking the two blocks to his house.

Max ran past. When he saw Jordan, he stopped. Screwing up his face, he waved his arms wildly. Then he laughed, stuck out his tongue, and ran on.

Jordan rubbed his sweaty palms on his jeans. What a jerk. He hated Max. And he was afraid of him. Home would be nice. He could practice kicking his soccer ball and read a Hardy Boys mystery.

He turned his key in the lock and opened the door. Jordan blew air through the space in his front teeth. "Pheei!" He could feel a sound. He wondered if other kids could make that sound too. Or was he special?

Chapter 3

The next day, Jordan dragged himself into the classroom. He'd had an awful fight with his parents the night before. About wanting to go to a school just for deaf kids.

But they'd both said, "No." *This town is too small. There aren't any deaf classes or schools here,* signed his mother.

You can adjust to new things, signed his father. *I'm adjusting to a new job.*

But you wanted come here, signed Jordan. *Not me!* He'd socked his fist into his other hand.

I needed this job, signed his father.

They'd both hugged him and offered to help. But his mother heard normally. So did his father. They couldn't really understand.

Being deaf wasn't difficult around other deaf kids. But it sure was in this class! He slumped into his seat and squinted his eyes.

A young woman came to him. She smelled of roses. Her eyes reflected the glow of her smile. She stood in front of him and signed.

11

I'm Sandy, your interpreter.

Jordan sat up straight.

Mr. Allrite came in and smiled at her. He said something to the class and pointed to her.

Then he spoke and Sandy signed what he said. *Good morning. Today we start with math again. Page 29. Do the division problems. I'll teach you to sign your names, one at a time.*

When Jordan watched Sandy, he couldn't watch Mr. Allrite. He tried to concentrate on the numbers on his paper. But he saw Abdul go to the teacher's desk.

Abdul stood in front of Mr. Allrite.

The teacher moved his hands and fingers.

Abdul moved his hands and fingers the same way.

Mr. Allrite nodded.

Abdul rubbed his fuzzy hair and grinned. He left the desk and another boy came up.

This went on all morning. A boy, a girl, two boys, three girls. When it was Lisa's turn, she shook her head.

Mr. Allrite went over to her desk. He signed, *Lisa.*

She looked away from him.

He took her hands in his. He moved them to spell her name.

Lisa pulled her hands away. She shook her head.

Jordan pushed his hair back. Of course she didn't want to sign. At oral school it wasn't allowed!

Exactly the opposite of his old school. Kids there talked only by signing and lip-reading. It showed pride in being deaf. It was a special language using hands instead of a voice. He'd

12

gotten along just fine. Until now.

Lisa was so cute with her brown eyes and long black hair. He wanted to be friends with her. Only how? He could sign in front of her. Lisa would close her eyes and jabber at him. He wouldn't hear what she said.

They'd make a silly pair. Of course, Sandy could sign to him and talk to Lisa. But that wouldn't be any fun.

Mr. Allrite patted Lisa's slim shoulder and went back to his desk.

It was Max's turn. He dashed to the desk. His orange ponytail flapped up and down as he copied Mr. Allrite's hand movements.

Then he dashed to Jordan's desk. *Hi. I'm Max*, he signed. He waved his hands in Jordan's face and burst out laughing. Then he sprinted away.

Jordan rubbed his knuckles. The person I don't like can sign, he thought. But the girl I like won't. The red light flashed for lunch.

Abdul ran over and stood facing Jordan.

Sandy signed what Abdul said. *Wanna' have lunch with me again?*

Jordan grinned and nodded. He liked Abdul even though they didn't really talk. This was so different than communicating with deaf friends.

Sandy signed, *See you later.* Then she left the room.

In the cafeteria, a girl came to Jordan and Abdul's table. Her curly brown braid hung down her back. Green eyes sparkled as she spoke. "I Rachel. Two years here from Russia. Still not talk English so good."

Jordan heard most of what she said. But her accent made it difficult to read her lips.

And what was that about Russia? Hey, he realized, that means she speaks another language—Russian.

The important thing was she wanted to be friends. How could he tell her enough signs to talk? He put his hand over his mouth and shook his head.

"Oh," she said. "You not speaking." She ran away from him.

That ends that, thought Jordan. I can't make friends here.

But the Russian girl came back—holding a notebook and pen. She wrote something. Then she gave the notebook to Jordan.

He read, My name is Rachel. How I tell you?

Jordan grinned. He pointed to the first sentence and signed it. Slowly, word by word.

Rachel copied his hand movements. Then she wrote in her notebook again. I like to be friends. Can you hear something?

He nodded and pointed to his left ear. This writing and pointing took so long! What if there was a fire?

Rachel would write, There's a fire in this room. He'd have to find the fire. He'd have to decide how to leave the room. They'd both have to fly above the fire. Or dig a tunnel out! There must be a faster way to communicate.

The weekend and three days passed. Most of the kids could sign *Hi*. Abdul and Rachel could sign other words too.

So could Max. But he used signing as a way to make fun of Jordan.

Lisa still didn't sign at all. Since that first day, she didn't come near Jordan.

Maybe she doesn't like me, he thought.

He couldn't accept this possibility. There must be a way to ask her, but she doesn't sign. I don't speak and I don't want Sandy's help. Then Jordan remembered writing with Rachel.

So he wrote in his notebook. Are you mad at me or what? Can we be friends? He held the notebook in front of Lisa.

She backed away.

Jordan touched her arm, then the page of writing.

Lisa looked at it. "Oh!" She bit her lips and shook her head.

Jordan didn't understand. Did Lisa mean she wasn't mad? Or that she didn't want to be friends? He handed her a pencil and waited nervously.

She wrote, I'm not mad. Then her lips parted and sounds came out. "Na- maa-d, no-t mad."

Jordan got the idea. He pointed to his eyes, her mouth.

She stood directly in front of him. She pointed to her eyes, his lips. "Sa-me," she said. "We ha-v the same prob-lem. Fr-iends. We can be fri-ends."

Jordan wrote, Please learn to sign so we can talk.

Lisa read the words. She put her hand over her mouth. She seemed to be thinking.

Jordan shifted from his right foot to his left. He shifted from his left foot to his right. He pulled his hair over his eyebrows. What would she decide?

Finally, Lisa took the notebook from him and wrote in it.

15

Jordan read, I'll learn to sign for you. You learn to speak for me. We will talk.

A tight lump filled Jordan's throat. He wanted Lisa for a friend. Could he possibly learn to use his voice?

Chapter 4

A few weeks later, Mr. Allrite made an announcement.

Sandy signed. *Our class has been asked to perform a Thanksgiving play for the whole school. We're going to write it this afternoon. So start thinking of story ideas.*

Jordan raised his hand. *What do you mean?* he signed. *Thanksgiving is about Pilgrims and Indians and food.*

Mr. Allrite adjusted his glasses.

Jordan watched Sandy sign the teacher's answer. *True. However, we could have a modern story. Or a funny one. It could still have the real meaning of Thanksgiving.*

Jordan nodded. He'd think up a funny story. That would make the kids laugh and he'd feel good again! Only... how would he <u>tell</u> his idea? Could the kids understand him yet?

All during math, Jordan rubbed his knuckles and worried. He worried during the beans-and-franks lunch. He worried while he raced Abdul and Rachel to the playground to play soccer. He wanted to get a funny idea.

The next day, he was back to worrying. How would he tell his funny idea after he got it?

He remembered "talking" with Rachel. She had written to him. Another time, he had written to Lisa. "Talking" on paper...sure! The kids would read the words and understand.

At morning recess, Jordan sat on a damp wooden bench behind a maple tree. What could be funny about Thanksgiving? Pilgrims? A turkey? Indians?

Jordan pushed his hair from his eyes. He breathed in the pungent smells of October— rotting walnuts, fallen apples. He pictured a Pilgrim man asking an Indian man how to plant corn.

The Pilgrim speaks English. The Indian doesn't understand him. How can they talk to each other? Suddenly, Jordan had a great idea. He hurried back to the classroom and started to write.

Other kids came in. Rachel tapped him on the shoulder. She pointed to the front of the room.

Mr. Allrite was talking. Sandy interpreted. *Write your story ideas. I'll collect them before we go home. Oh. Don't put your names on the papers. We'll vote on ideas, not on who wrote them.*

Jordan wrote one page. The red light flashed for lunch. He noticed a girl with tiny braids all over her head. She wore a matching top and pants outfit. She was new in their class.

Her nose pointed into the air. She took

18

small steps close behind Lisa and then poked Lisa's back.

Strange, thought Jordan, and kind of weird.

After lunch the girl poked Lisa again.

What was going on? Jordan moved closer so he could read their lips.

Lisa turned around. "Stop hurt-ing me," she said.

The nasty girl pointed to Lisa's back. "You're a slob," she said.

Rachel rushed over and looked. "Button open." She stood in front of Lisa. "I can fix." She rebuttoned the blouse and patted Lisa's shoulder. She signed, okay, to Jordan.

But the new girl wasn't through being nasty. She smirked at Rachel. "You need lessons in dressing too. Such weird clothes." She poked Rachel's striped dress.

Rachel pushed the girl's hand away and smoothed her dress. With tear-filled eyes, she spoke. "What do you mean, Sabrina?"

Jordan saw what they said. He saw Rachel's tears. He wanted to sock Sabrina.

Before he could, Max rushed up. "Dummies!" he yelled at Lisa and Rachel.

Sabrina smiled at Max. She pointed at Lisa. Then she turned around and pointed at Jordan. "Deafies."

Abdul came in front of Jordan. "Let's get 'em!" He shoved Sabrina away from the other girls.

Now Jordan flew into action. He punched Max in the stomach. Then he pushed him down.

The playground teacher rushed over, blowing her whistle.

19

Sabrina grabbed Max's arm. She pulled him up and away from the other kids.

"What's going on here?" demanded the teacher.

"Nothing," said Sabrina.

The teacher scowled. "Well, I'll be watching you." She left.

Max hunched over, holding his stomach and glared up at Jordan.

"C'mon," said Sabrina. "Let's get out of here. We'll get even later."

Abdul told Jordan what everyone said. Then he grinned and shook Jordan's hand.

Lisa and Rachel smiled at their heroes. All four friends went back to class.

Jordan finished writing his play idea.

Mr. Allrite collected the kids' papers. He waved as the kids left the room.

On the way home, Jordan watched out for Max. But he wasn't in sight.

Jordan took off his school shirt and pulled on a soft T-shirt. He smiled. School was much better. Abdul, Rachel, Lisa and him, four friends. Against Max and Sabrina.

The next afternoon, Mr. Allrite waved a hand filled with papers. Sandy interpreted. *I read many good play ideas. Now get into groups of four or five so we can read them.*

Boys and girls popped out of their seats. They looked at each other for a second or two. Then they scrambled around, finding friends.

Jordan flipped his FM on and stood up. Suddenly, Rachel, Lisa and Abdul were by his side. They grinned at each other.

Mr. Allrite handed several papers to each group. Sandy signed his words. *Read and*

20

choose the one you like best. I'll read your favorites out loud. Then the class will vote.

Jordan understood. He hoped his would be chosen. Which pile was it in?

The four friends gathered around Jordan's desk. Rachel sat next to him on one side, Lisa on the other. Abdul looked over his shoulder. Sandy stayed nearby in case he needed her.

The first idea was good. They giggled over the next idea. The last one was dumb.

By mid-afternoon, each committee had chosen a favorite. Mr. Allrite collected the papers.

Ten-minute recess, signed Sandy. *I have to leave. Your teacher will sign.*

After recess, Mr. Allrite started to read. But both his hands were on the papers. He didn't sign.

Jordan rubbed his knuckles hard. He could only hear some words. His teacher was looking down, so it was impossible to lipread. How would he know if his idea was chosen?

He wanted to sign something. But the teacher wouldn't see him. He wished he could really speak.

"Mi-ter All-ri-te!" Lisa exclaimed.

The teacher jerked in surprise. Papers flew out of his hands like rockets. They zoomed around, then plunged to the floor. He looked at Lisa.

"You a-re not sii-ning," she said.

Jordan felt a warm glow inside. Lisa understands, he thought.

Mr. Allrite walked to a corner of the room. He returned with a metal music stand.

Rachel and Abdul scooped up the papers

21

and gave them to the teacher.

He put the papers on the stand. Then he pushed up his glasses and signed with empty hands. *Let's try again.* His lips moved too.

Jordan watched his teacher's mouth and hands. He listened to the sounds. They were easier to understand now because of his friend Lisa. He took a deep breath. He recognized some words. It was his paper Mr. Allrite was reading!

The kids smiled. Their mouths opened with laughter and they clapped!

Mr. Allrite read the other papers. Even with signing and the FM, Jordan had an awful time understanding the ideas. He really needed Sandy.

Then Mr. Allrite used the overhead projector. He wrote numbers from one to seven. *Raise your hands if you chose number one,* he signed.

Two kids raised their hands.

Number two?

Four kids raised their hands.

Jordan's heart thumped faster. They would vote on his idea next. He made a vow. If he won, he'd go to speech therapy with Lisa. Then his friends could understand him easier.

The teacher pointed to the overhead. "Number three?" he asked.

Jordan held his breath. Only one hand was raised.

Chapter 5

But then another hand went up. And another. And another!

Jordan counted. Four, five...eight...twelve ...seventeen. Almost everybody in the class!

Mr. Allrite laughed. *I can see which one's winning,* he signed and said. *But we'll vote anyway. Number four.*

Soon the voting ended—and Sandy returned. Jordan's idea had the most votes. She signed, *Number three wins.* The kids were clapping.

Jordan grinned with happiness.

Mr. Allrite spoke. Sandy signed his words. *Whose idea is number three?*

Jordan felt his grin drop. If the kids knew...they might stop clapping. They might make fun of him. Fear froze his body. I won't tell, he thought. Maybe in a few days....

Mr. Allrite looked puzzled. Then he smiled. *Well, I guess we have a secret writer.*

Secret writer, Jordan thought. Pride warmed his face. He took a deep breath and

23

remembered his vow. He would learn to speak. Starting today.

Jordan, Abdul, Lisa and Rachel sat hunched over their cafeteria lunches. Cheese macaroni, lima beans, biscuits and apples.

Sabrina and Max walked to their table.

Jordan saw their lips moving. He couldn't hear what they said. I don't trust them, he thought.

Max came closer to Rachel's tray. His skinny arm reached out. He grabbed her apple.

Sabrina grabbed Jordan's and ran away.

Now Max reached for Lisa's apple. Abdul jumped up. He karatied Max's arm. Max stuck out his tongue and ran after Sabrina.

Two apples were gone. Rachel cut her apple and gave half to Lisa.

Abdul gave half of his to Jordan. He faced Lisa and Jordan. "Those troublemakers can't be trusted." He pointed across the playground to Max and Sabrina.

Lisa and Rachel nodded.

Jordan wished he could say something. But he didn't know how. There was still some lunch recess time. He left his friends and went to the classroom.

Mr. Allrite sat at his desk eating a sandwich. The aroma of salami and garlic wafted around him. *Hello, Jordan,* he signed. *What do you need?*

I want to learn to speak. Where is the speech therapist?

Try room 42—at the end of the hall. Good luck, signed his teacher.

Jordan went to speech therapy three times that week. He learned to say "Yes" and "No."

Mr. Allrite helped the class write the play story. He went to the overhead projector. As he spoke, Sandy signed. *We want to show early Indians and Pilgrims. How they communicated with each other. What funny things could happen?*

Several hands went up. Mr. Allrite called on one kid at a time. He wrote what each said on the overhead. Planting corn. Chopping wood. Getting lost in a forest.

The words helped Jordan understand what the kids were saying. But it was difficult to watch Sandy at the same time.

Where should the play start? asked his teacher. *Which town? How many days before Thanksgiving? What kind of weather?*

Jordan couldn't follow the discussion. Even with his interpreter's help, it was too fast. He rubbed his knuckles. His idea! Anger pounded through his body and he opened his mouth and yelled. "No!"

The kids stared at him. Mr. Allrite shrugged. *Sorry*, he signed. *Are you the secret writer?*

Jordan was so angry, he didn't care who knew. "Yes-ss!" He blew the word out through the space between his front teeth.

The kids looked surprised.

Mr. Allrite laughed. He spoke and Sandy signed. *I'm glad you're the secret writer. And you just whistled! Can you do it again?*

Jordan squirmed in his seat. Whistle? That strange feeling he had when he blew through his front teeth? He did it again and the kids clapped.

All the way home, Jordan whistled. He

25

thought, the playground teacher has a whistle. It must be loud because I can hear her blow it. He realized that he made the same sound! And the kids liked it. He was popular, like at his old school. Happiness spread over him like grape jelly on an English muffin.

Suddenly, Max darted from behind a tree. "Deafie!" he shouted. He waved his arms and stuck out his tongue.

Deaf is good, thought Jordan. I can whistle. He blew through his teeth.

Max stopped waving. He puckered up his mouth and blew.

Jordan heard nothing. No loud sound. No scritchy sound.

Max blew until his face puffed out and became red. Still no sound came out—Max couldn't whistle!

Jordan walked past him. At home, he ate the peanut butter cookies and milk his mother prepared. He went into his bedroom and picked up the Hardy Boys book. He was almost finished reading it.

Jordan whistled as he turned to the last chapter. How many kids whistle like me? he wondered. Is my way special?

Chapter 6

The next morning, Jordan whistled his way to school.

Lisa stood at Mr. Allrite's desk, in front of him.

The teacher moved his hands and fingers.

Lisa copied him. She was learning to sign!

Hey, thought Jordan. Soon we can talk to each other like real friends.

Sandy came into the room and class started. Mr. Allrite turned on the overhead projector. *In order to get our play ready, we'll need to work in four committees. This is what I figured.*

Jordan heard sounds through his FM receiver. He watched Sandy signing. He also read the teacher's lips. Sounds were beginning to make more sense. He looked at the overhead writing.

1. Dialogue committee: Decide how many characters. Write what they say and do.

2. Costume committee: What did Pilgrims wear? What did Indians wear? Find information and pictures from history books. Check in

school library.

3. Scenery committee: Paint background landscapes for each act. Use weather, trees, birds and animals.

4. Prop committee: Write down what actors will need. Guns, bows and arrows, etc. Maybe tables and chairs? Plan how to get them.

"Okay, choose your committees now." The kids rushed to the four corners of the room. One corner for each committee. Jordan chose the prop committee and Rachel, Abdul and Lisa joined him.

Every afternoon for the next two weeks, the kids worked in their committees. Jordan's group made a list of props. All the ones that might be needed in the play.

He ate lunch with his friends in the cafeteria. Afterward, they kicked the soccer ball around.

One Friday, the red light blinked, as usual, for lunch. Jordan saw Sabrina poke Rachel's back.

Rachel turned around and smiled.

Uh, oh, thought Jordan. Sabrina's up to something.

She opened her mouth, making sounds. Then she laughed and ran from the room.

Rachel's face crumpled. Tears rolled from her eyes. Lisa rushed over to hug Rachel.

Jordan came closer to the girls. He touched Lisa's hand. *What's wrong?* he signed.

She pointed after Sabrina and shook her head. Then she spoke slowly. "Sa-bri-na said Ra-chel was a dumb fo-reigner."

I'm sorry, he signed to Rachel.

She nodded and signed, *Thanks.* "I talk Russian at home and it's easy," she said. "This English at school is hard. I don't always understand."

Hey, Rachel feels like me, thought Jordan. Signing is easy. Speaking English is very difficult.

But he wanted to communicate better with his friends. So after lunch he didn't play soccer. He went back to the classroom.

Mr. Allrite was eating his lunch. *What's up?* he signed.

I want to speak better, Jordan signed. *Speech class isn't enough.   want to practice with you every day. Okay?*

His teacher nodded.

So every lunch recess Jordan practiced speaking with Mr. Allrite. And every morning before school Lisa practiced signing with him.

Finally, Jordan and Lisa could talk to each other. "No. He-lo. Goodbye." They signed to each other. *Than-ks.   Co-mm. You are my friend.*

On Monday afternoon, Sandy signed and Mr. Allrite spoke. *Class, we're ready to cast our play. Who wants a speaking part?*

Fifteen kids raised their hands.

Sadness washed over Jordan like waves on wet sand. I want to be in our play, he thought. It's from my idea. But I can't talk enough. He didn't raise his hand.

Neither did Rachel. Nor Lisa. But Abdul raised his hand. So did Max and Sabrina.

Mr. Allrite motioned them to his desk. He handed each of them a copy of the play.

Jordan listened and lipread. He tried to

29

watch Sandy sign.

Choose one character and study the lines. Tomorrow each of you will read out loud and the rest of us will listen. Remember. Actors must have loud voices.

Suddenly, Lisa raised her hand. "I have a loud voice," she said.

Mr. Allrite pushed up his glasses. "You certainly do." He gave her a script.

"I'll be an old lady Pilgrim," she said to Jordan.

The next afternoon, Mr. Allrite came to Jordan. He signed, *I want you to listen when each kid reads. If you hear sounds, raise your hand. Sandy won't be signing.*

I don't understand, signed Jordan. *Why?*

Mr. Allrite grinned. *People come to watch the play. These people need to hear the actors. If you hear sounds, they hear words. Okay?*

Jordan squirmed in his seat. He hoped the kids wouldn't call him "teacher's pet." But he liked Mr. Allrite. So he said, "Yes."

Lisa and Sabrina were easy for Jordan to hear. They chose parts as Pilgrim women.

Abdul made a good Indian chief. Some kids read Pilgrim parts. Some read Indian parts. Whenever Jordan heard sounds, he raised his hand.

Suddenly, it was Max's turn. He walked to the front of the room. He shifted from one foot to the other and chewed his lips. He opened and closed his mouth.

Jordan couldn't hear him. What a surprise! Max usually waved his arms and shouted. But now he was quiet and his face turned pale. Was Max afraid in front of the whole class?

30

If he doesn't get a part, he'll get angry at me. Jordan rubbed his knuckles. He struggled with his feelings. Fear of Max. Wanting the play to be good.

Finally, Jordan shrugged. He couldn't hear Max, so he didn't raise his hand.

"Sorry, Max," said Mr. Allrite while Sandy signed. *There's things you can do instead of acting. Tomorrow we'll measure the actors for costumes.*

After school, Abdul ran in front of Jordan. *Can I come to your house?* he gestured. *We could play soccer.*

Jordan smiled. He hadn't played soccer for several days. It would be fun. "Yes," he said.

Max jumped out of some bushes. "I would've been an Indian!" he shouted. "You didn't want me!"

Chapter 7

Jordan exchanged a look with Abdul. "He's got a loud voice now," said Abdul.

"Weirdos!" Max waved his arms and dashed away.

"Jerk," said Jordan. "Let's play ball." He ran toward his house. His friend ran with him.

At school the next afternoon, Mr. Allrite held up a bronze bell. He shook it in the air. "Attention," he said.

He put the bell on his desk. He pointed to a pile of fabrics. He spoke and Sandy signed. *We'll make costumes. The costume committee's in charge. I hope some parents can help.*

Jordan watched his teacher unfold the fabrics. Smooth blue, lumpy gray and rough brown. *The PTA donated the money for these,* Sandy signed. *We'll use the materials to make Pilgrim costumes.*

Mr. Allrite took a box from under his desk. *Here's stuff for Indian costumes. Actors, come get what you need.*

Abdul hurried over to the box. He lifted out

a feathered headdress. Max dashed up and clutched it.

Max isn't in the play, thought Jordan. Doesn't need feathers! He was so angry he leaped from his seat. He grabbed the stiff headdress from Max.

He put it on Abdul's head. "Cheee-fff," he said.

Abdul grinned and patted the brown-speckled feathers.

Max glared at them. He shook his fist and stamped away.

Lisa and Sabrina walked to the pile of cloth. They both reached for the same blue piece. Sabrina pulled it away from Lisa and wrapped it around herself. She made a face at Lisa.

Lisa stamped her foot. "I need that!" She grabbed one end of the cloth off Sabrina. She wrapped it around herself.

Sabrina grabbed back. And, suddenly, there they were—stuck together.

Uh, oh, thought Jordan. I should help Lisa.

But Rachel beat him to it. She scooped a giant pair of scissors from Mr. Allrite's desk. Then she ran to the two stuck girls and started cutting them apart.

"No, no," shouted their teacher.

He shook the brass bell with one hand. He waved a tape measure with the other.

Rachel stopped cutting. She looked at Mr. Allrite.

So did Jordan. Then he looked around the room.

Other kids were stuck together too! In gray

cloth. In brown cloth. In other pieces of blue.

Mr. Allrite pointed at them. "Unwind," he commanded.

All the kids pulled at the same second. They tangled and fell into each other. Specks of dust flew into the air.

Jordan burst out laughing.

Mr. Allright shook the bell again.

The kids stood still, even Lisa and Sabrina. The dust specks settled to the floor.

Help me, the teacher signed to Jordan. He motioned to another boy and girl. The four of them unrolled the kids from the cloth pieces.

Mr. Allrite laughed with everyone. He spoke and Sandy signed. *Before cutting, you need to measure.*

He placed the cloth tape on Lisa's waist and stretched it to the floor. He wrote "27 inches" on the overhead. *It should be this long for Lisa's Pilgrim skirt.*

He motioned to Sabrina. *Measure Lisa's waist.*

Sabrina wrapped the tape around Lisa. She pulled it tight.

"Oo-ww," yelled Lisa.

Take it easy! Mr. Allrite took the tape away from Sabrina. He wrote "24 inches" on the overhead. 24 x 2—*The skirt should be this wide before sewing. Then it will be gathered at the waist.*

He reached into the box and pulled out a faded red-and-brown blanket. He gave it to Abdul.

Then Mr. Allrite handed each costume committee member a tape measure. *Get busy.*

Some kids started measuring and cutting.

35

Others pulled out more blankets from the box. Green-and-tan, yellow-and-brown, red-and-blue.

Jordan ran to Abdul. He folded a blanket around him. But it was way too big even for his tall friend.

It covered his arms and head and dragged on the floor. Abdul couldn't walk.

Jordan pulled him to Mr. Allrite's desk. *I need scissors,* he signed.

The teacher held the blanket while Jordan cut.

Abdul grinned. He wiggled his feet and took a step. The blanket fell off.

Mr. Allrite handed Jordan some big safety pins.

Jordan stuck them into the blanket.

Abdul tried walking again. This time, the blanket stayed on.

"Yes!" said Jordan.

The next two days were spent making costumes. Two mothers and one father helped. They threaded needles and showed kids how to sew. They stapled some costumes.

On Thursday, Mr. Allrite motioned to the prop committee. *Come to Jordan's desk.*

Jordan got out the list of props. Rachel and the teacher came to his desk. "Lee-sa," called Jordan. "Ab-duul."

Lisa hurried over. Her blue Pilgrim skirt dragged along the floor. "My cos-tuu-me is not done," she said.

Mr. Allrite laughed. "I see," he said. He motioned her to go back.

Abdul rushed over wearing the red-and-brown blanket.

How can he help? Jordan signed and pointed

to Abdul's pinned-in arms.

Mr. Allrite shook his head and Sandy signed his words. *You need kids who aren't actors.* He called across the room.

Max sprinted over, frowning.

A short, blue-eyed girl walked to Jordan's desk. *My name is Kris*, she signed.

She's okay, thought Jordan. But Max will make trouble.

Chapter 8

Mr. Allrite looked at the list of props needed. Guns, bows and arrows, table, cooking pots. "Good start," he said. He handed scripts to Jordan and Rachel.

Sandy signed his next words. *Go through the script. Make a list of "hand" props. Actors hold these during the play. Then make a list of "set" props—like table and chairs. Do it for each act.*

Rachel and Jordan put four desks together into a square. She sat next to Kris. He sat next to Max.

Max grabbed the script from Jordan's hands. "I'll tell you what we need," he said.

Jordan grabbed it back. "No!" he said.

Kris said something that Jordan couldn't hear. He tried to read her lips because he didn't want help from Sandy. Finally, he wrote in a notebook. Loud pop? Why?

She shook her head and smiled. Then she spoke slower and pointed to each of the kids. "We can read the props out loud." She pointed

39

to Jordan and, *you write.*

He nodded. But, he thought, I might not hear all the words. I'd write down the wrong prop. He looked at the other committee members.

Rachel doesn't always understand and I don't trust Max. He pointed to Kris and gestured. *You write the words.*

Okay, she signed back. She stood up and walked across the room. She came back with a pen and paper.

Rachel and Max read the script aloud page by page.

Jordan raised his hand each time they came to a hand prop.

Kris wrote it down.

Rachel said, "How will we get so many?"

"Stupid," said Max. "We'll buy them."

Mr. Allrite walked to their group. "Is there a problem?"

Do we have money for props? signed Jordan.

Their teacher shook his head. "You can borrow some and make the rest." He walked to his desk.

Kris stuck her tongue out at Max. Rachel said, "You the stupid one." Jordan grinned.

After school, Max did his leap out of the bushes. He even ran around Jordan, making faces.

Jordan didn't like this at all. Sweat trickled down his neck. His mouth felt dry. He didn't want to fight. So he walked quickly past this obnoxious boy.

Max stuck out his tongue. Then he ran in

40

a different direction. Soon he was out of sight.

Abdul rushed alongside. "Want company?"

Jordan nodded. They walked to his house.

"Want to play soccer?" asked Abdul.

Jordan smiled and nodded again.

His mother gave them orange juice and ginger cookies. The two friends demolished the food.

Then they ran to the backyard with Jordan's soccer ball. They kicked the ball. They practiced headers.

The next day, Mr. Allrite brought several stiff sheets of white posterboard to class. He handed them to Jordan. "You can use these to make hand props," he said. Sandy signed, *You're in charge.*

Max frowned. "How can you be in charge?" he said. "You're deaf."

Kris and Rachel took out their pencils. They placed a sheet of posterboard over the four desks. They tried to draw on it, but it wobbled.

Rachel faced Jordan. "Not good," she said.

Kris smoothed the posterboard with her hand. Jordan read her lips. "You're wrong. This posterboard's okay."

Rachel shook her head. "Not good to draw." She pushed down on the sheet and it bent.

Kris's face turned pink.

Uh, oh, thought Jordan. Kris thinks Rachel means posterboard won't work. But Rachel means it needs a different place.

He picked up the sheet and carried it to a large corner table. The others followed.

Rachel pushed down on the sheet and it stayed straight. She smiled. "Now okay to draw."

41

Kris laughed. "Okay, I get it!" she said.

Max frowned and mumbled something. Jordan couldn't hear him or read his lips.

Then Max started to draw with a soft pencil. He drew a rifle and a long arrow. They looked wonderful! He put his pencil down and walked away.

Jordan stood still. One gun and one arrow. Not nearly enough! *Can you draw?* he gestured to Rachel. She shook her head. So did Kris. I can't draw either, he thought. But Max really could. Why won't he stick to it?

Jordan rested his elbow on the table and propped up his head, thinking. What now? He glanced around the room.

The costume makers were cutting fabric. Scissors! He got a pair from Mr. Allrite's desk.

He cut out the rifle and the arrow. He said, "We ne-ed mo-re."

Kris laid the arrow on the posterboard. She drew around it. She cut it out. *Okay?* she signed.

Jordan nodded happily.

Rachel laid the rifle on the posterboard. She drew around it. Kris cut it out.

"Yes," said Jordan. He took the rifle and arrow to Abdul. *Try the gun*, he gestured.

Abdul pretended to shoot. *Okay*, he signed. He picked up the arrow. *Where's the bow?* he gestured.

Jordan shook his head. He took the cardboard props back to the table. He wrote on a piece of paper and showed it to Rachel and Kris. We need to make a bow.

Kris rushed to the Indian information books. She brought one to their table. She found a picture of a bow used by the Wampanoag tribe. This was the Indian tribe that the Pilgrims knew. She showed the picture to Jordan and Rachel.

Rachel measured the arrow. Fifteen inches, she wrote.

The three of them worked together drawing a bow.

"Need string," said Rachel. They found a roll of kite string in one box.

Jordan notched the bow at top and bottom. He cut a piece of string. He attached it to the bow. He put in the arrow. It fell out. He put it in again. It fell out again. Put in—fall out. Not good at all!

Kris picked up the arrow and notched both ends. She put the arrow between bow and string. "Now try it."

They rushed this prop to Abdul for testing.

He held the bow. Pulled the string toward his chest. Zing! The arrow shot forward, then fell.

Sandy came to sign Abdul's words. *You couldn't catch a rabbit dinner. But maybe a slow turkey.*

Jordan laughed. They needed to make enough rifles and arrows for all the actors.

Max didn't come back to school that week.

Jordan wondered, Is Max sick? Maybe he just doesn't want to help us. With Rachel and Kris, he outlined fish, pumpkins and turkeys. They cut them out.

After school, Abdul spoke to Jordan. "My birthday's coming," he said. "I'm asking for a soccer ball. Then we can play at my house."

Jordan grinned. Soon both of them would

be the best soccer players in fourth grade!

At school, rehearsals continued. In between, Lisa came to Jordan. "Tee-ch me mo-re s-i-gns," she said. She pointed to her mouth. Pretended to talk.

Jordan signed, *speak*.

She copied him, *speak*. *You speak*, she signed. "Sp-ea-k," she said.

Jordan tried. "S-ea," he said.

Lisa shook her head. "Lo-ok a-t me. Sp-ea-k." She smiled and patted his arm.

Sweat trickled from Jordan's forehead. He was proud to be deaf and sign. His back tensed up. Why bother talking?

Chapter 9

Jordan looked at Lisa's cute face. She'd signed for him. She was his friend. That's why she wanted him to talk. He tried once more. "Spe-ea—ckk," he said.

Lisa clapped her hands and laughed.

Rachel and Abdul raced to him and patted him on the back.

Jordan grinned. Speaking was hard work. But it made his friends happier—and he didn't care about his enemies.

On Monday, Max came back. "Where's the props?" he yelled.

Jordan rubbed his knuckles. He really didn't feel like having anything to do with this guy. But there were a lot of props to paint. So he showed Max the box of posterboard pumpkins, turkeys, guns, arrows and bows.

Rachel came over. She frowned at Max. "We needed you for drawing," she said.

Kris appeared, glaring at Max. "Better stick around," she said.

"Can't get by without me?" he snickered.

45

Jordan wanted to punch him again.

But Mr. Allrite waved them to his desk. Sandy came and signed the teacher's words. *Take the props to the art room. Paint there today and tomorrow.*

Jordan and his committee went to the art room. They found orange and green paint for the pumpkins. They found brown for the rifles and bows. There was red paint to add to the turkeys.

"Try not to get the bow strings wet," said Kris.

Max grabbed a brush. He slapped orange on a pumpkin. Paint spattered on the floor, the chairs—and Rachel's blue blouse.

Kris stamped her foot. "Stop it!" she shouted.

Rachel looked at her orange-spattered blouse. Tears filled her eyes.

Hot anger filled Jordan. Max had no right to act this way. "Go!" he shouted.

Max threw down his brush and walked out of the room.

But a few minutes later he slunk back, like a scolded dog. Mr. Allrite marched behind him. The teacher looked at the spatters. He walked to the sink and got soapy sponges and pushed them into Max's hands. "Clean up," he said, "right now." Jordan could hear Mr. Allrite and read his lips.

The teacher turned to Rachel. "When you get home, wash your blouse in cold water," he said. "I think those spots will come out."

The next day, Max didn't come to the art room.

Rachel lifted a bow out to paint. The string

46

hung loose. "Maybe I can fix string," she said.

"Wait a minute," said Kris, touching the end. "Jordan, look at this!" she called.

He looked at the bowstring. Cut!

Rachel took out another bow. That string was cut too.

Jordan pulled out the rest of the bows. Every single string hung loose. Max must have done this. I'll get even with him, thought Jordan. I won't let that jerk ruin our class play.

There was no point complaining to Mr. Allrite. They couldn't really prove who cut the string. But Jordan knew. So did Rachel and Kris. The three of them retied the bows. They finished painting them.

Then they went back to the classroom to list the "set" props. "You read the script," said Kris. "I'll write—like we did before."

Jordan and Rachel nodded.

Max sat down next to Jordan. *I will write,* he signed.

Jordan drew in his breath. Max was an artist. He could even sign when he wanted to. Jordan knew they couldn't trust him. But Max had been assigned to their group. At least they could check his writing later....

Jordan nodded.

Kris gave the paper and pencil to Max. She and Rachel took turns reading.

Each time a set prop was needed, Jordan raised his hand.

"Act one. Benches or chairs on Mayflower. Plymouth rock.

"Act two. Blankets, snow, table, chairs, empty food sacks.

"Act three, nothing.

47

"Act four. Leaves, long table, chairs, food platters."

Max finished writing and folded the paper. He put it into his jeans pocket.

Jordan reached out his hand. *Give me the list*, he gestured.

Max stood up with the list still in his pocket. Didn't he understand?

"Jordan needs list," said Rachel.

Max turned to leave.

Kris grabbed one of his arms and Rachel grabbed the other.

Jordan stuck his hand into Max's pocket. He pulled out the list and looked at it. Act 1—rock. Act 2—snow. Act 3—zero. Act 4—food. "No good!" he exclaimed.

Rachel and Kris let go of Max. They looked at the list, too.

"Quick," said Rachel, facing Jordan. "Me and Kris can say all props. You can make new list before we forget."

Jordan ran to get Sandy. This time he wanted her help. He watched her sign what Rachel and Kris said. Then he wrote the list.

This was a real challenge—watching and writing at the same time. But he did it.

Now he had to get even with Max. For cutting the bows, splashing paint, and the unfinished list! Jordan looked around, but his enemy had disappeared.

Jordan showed the list to Mr. Allrite.

The teacher signed, *We have a table. We can borrow chairs, platters and blankets. Your committee could make Plymouth rock, snow and leaves. Abdul and Lisa can help again.*

All my friends are back, thought Jordan.

48

What if Max comes too? I can't let him. What should I do?

Several kids were drawing scenery. An idea flashed in Jordan's mind. He rushed to his teacher and tapped him on the arm. *Mr. Allrite*, he signed, *Max draws like an artist.*

Great! I'll get him to work on scenery.

Jordan heaved a sigh. Goodbye, Max, he thought. He went to the work table.

Rachel and Kris were already there. Abdul and Lisa ran up.

"Wha-t should we do?" asked Lisa.

"Make snow and leaves," said Rachel.

"And Plymouth Rock," said Kris.

The five of them sat, thinking. Suddenly, Lisa said, "Soa-pp."

"What say?" asked Abdul.

Jordan felt as confused as his friend looked. They were trying to think of ideas for snow and leaves. What did soap have to do with it?

"My mother has..." Lisa pressed her lips together. She rubbed her head. "Sno-fflaa-kes!" she exclaimed. She waved her arms and wiggled her fingers. "S-now-fla-kes fall-ing. So-ap."

This didn't make sense to Jordan. Maybe he better get Sandy.

"Wait," said Rachel. "Snow...soap...soap flakes?"

Lisa nodded. "My mo-ther has so-ap flakes!"

Jordan grinned. "Goo-d idea," he said.

Lisa smiled and smiled. "I will bring th-em."

"Now what about leaves?" asked Kris.

Rachel went to look out the window. The others followed her. There were lots of leaves out there. They could bring bags and collect some.

After school, Jordan whistled his way home. The props were coming along fine. And he could communicate easier with his friends.

The next day, Lisa brought a huge box of soapflakes. She put it in a corner of the room, under a table.

Then the prop committee went outdoors. Crisp red, brown, and golden leaves covered the ground.

A perfect day, thought Jordan. He gathered an armful of rustling leaves and pushed them into a big paper bag.

Each friend filled a bag too. They brought the bags into the classroom, next to the soap box.

Jordan noticed Max watching them and talking to Sabrina. I can't see their lips, he thought. But they're up to something!

Chapter 10

The light flashed for lunch. Jordan wanted to take the leaves and soapbox with him. He didn't trust Max—or Sabrina.

But Mr. Allrite usually stayed in the room or locked the door. Jordan thought everything would be all right.

As he followed Abdul, Jordan blew through his teeth.

His friend stopped walking and faced him. "Great whistle," he said. "Would you teach me how?"

After lunch Jordan showed Abdul how to whistle. But his friend had a problem. He didn't have a space between his front teeth like Jordan did. *You have to whistle another way,* signed Jordan.

Abdul shrugged and signed. *I don't understand.*

Jordan was stuck. He liked Abdul very much. His friend really wanted to whistle. But Jordan's way didn't work for him. What would?

The two boys ran to the soccer field.

Abdul pointed to another boy. "He's whistling too!"

Jordan couldn't hear anything, but he watched. The boy pursed his lips. *Try that*, he signed to Abdul.

His friend pursed his lips and blew. Again and again and again. He shrugged. "This blowing could fill twenty balloons." Abdul pursed his lips once more.

Jordan could imagine all those balloons. Here, there, everywhere! He started laughing.

Abdul and the other boy stared at him.

Jordan gestured with his arms. The boys shook their heads.

Suddenly, a green balloon floated by. Jordan pointed. He gestured again. *Balloons here, there, everywhere*. The boys watched in amazement.

Was Jordan a magician? He didn't think so. But then how...? He looked around. Oh.

A little girl stood on the other side of the school fence. She pointed to the balloon—now high in the sky. Her mother picked her up. They both waved to the disappearing balloon.

Jordan felt a tap on his shoulder.

Abdul and the other boy waved at the tiny green speck.

They all laughed.

"Class time," said Abdul, "and I can't whistle yet." He and Jordan went to their room.

Mr. Allrite was just opening the door. Without a key. He hadn't locked it!

The soap box was empty. So were the bags.

"Where the soap flakes?" asked Rachel.

Where are the leaves? Lisa signed.

Kris pointed to the floor. Bits of red, orange

and brown made a trail from the bags to the window.

The five of them ran to look out the window. They saw Max and Sabrina jumping and stamping on a pile of leaves. Their leaves!

Abdul knocked on the window. He shook his fist at the two enemies. So did Jordan.

Sabrina stared at them. She grabbed Max's arm.

He looked up and laughed. The two of them ran out of sight.

"They too-k our so-ap too," cried Lisa. "No more a-t home."

Rachel and Kris hugged her. Abdul patted her shoulder.

Jordan burned inside. His friend Lisa was crying. It's all my fault, he thought. It wasn't smart to leave the props. How can we get more in time?

"I'm off this committee," said Kris. "I'm gonna do something else."

The four friends looked at each other. Should they tell Mr. Allrite? Could he help? Or should they handle this themselves?

The teacher came into the room with Sabrina and Max. He marched them to Jordan and his friends. Sandy came over and signed his words. *These two took your leaves and soapflakes.*

The four friends nodded. They knew this already. They just didn't know what to do.

I phoned Max's parents. They'll send another box of soapflakes tomorrow. The teacher handed Sabrina and Max the empty bags. *Go outside and fill them.*

It's okay now, signed Abdul. Rachel and

Lisa smiled.

But Jordan shook his head. "Max will ma-ke more t-rouble," he said. "Can't le-t him!"

Lisa said, "We will wa-tch hi-m."

"And we watch Sabrina," said Rachel. "She makes trouble too."

"We can take turns," said Abdul.

Jordan heard and lipread what they said. *Good idea,* he signed.

The dismissal light flashed. Abdul rushed to Jordan. "My birthday's this weekend. I hope I get that soccer ball."

Jordan heard most of the words. He wished his friend was having a party. But not all kids had birthday parties.

On Monday, Abdul carried two bags with handles. They looked heavy, so Jordan raced over to help.

"What's inside?" asked Rachel.

Abdul opened one bag. "Chocolate chip cookies for the class."

"Yumm," said Lisa. "Wha-t is in the o-ther?"

Abdul grinned. "Show you at recess."

Jordan hoped it was a soccer ball. And it was. Brand new and shiny. "Can we play with it?" he asked Abdul.

His friend nodded. "You and me. Rachel and Lisa too."

After lunch the four of them ran out to the soccer field. Abdul kicked his new ball to Rachel. She swung her foot forward and up. The ball soared high.

Jordan ran under it and used his head to knock the ball to Lisa. She kicked it hard and it rolled along the ground. Abdul raced forward.

Suddenly, Max sprinted across the soccer field and kicked the ball away from Abdul. He ran after it and kicked again. Hard and high.

It soared over the fence and into the street. Just as a cement-mixer truck roared around the corner.

Chapter 11

The four friends ran to the fence. They watched in horror as a heavy tire hit Abdul's ball. Pow! The truck rolled on.

A flattened piece of leather lay on the street.

Abdul stared at the disaster. Jordan and the others didn't know what to do.

"Lose something?" It was Max.

Rachel yelled, "You did this!"

With her fists, Lisa pounded on Max's chest.

He shouted something and pushed her away. He ran toward the building.

Jordan chased him. He'd make Max pay.

Max ran around the building. Jordan ran after him. Anger gave him the power to run faster than ever before. He focused on Max.

His enemy ran into the building. Jordan sprinted after him. And bumped into—Mr. Allrite!

His teacher grabbed him around the shoulders. He said something.

Jordan was too angry to listen. He struggled to get loose. He had to catch Max!

Mr. Allrite held him until he stopped struggling. Then he let go of Jordan and looked at him. *What's going on?* he signed.

Jordan rubbed his knuckles. He didn't want a grownup solving this problem. But he didn't want Max to get away with ruining Abdul's new ball. What should he do?

Before he thought up an answer, he saw his friends.

Rachel hurried down the hall toward him. Lisa and Abdul ran behind her.

"What's going on?" Mr. Allrite frowned. Then he looked at the four of them and sighed. "Your faces tell me it's really bad."

A tear rolled down Lisa's cheek. "Max did some-thin-g aw-ful," she said.

They all nodded.

"What happened?"

"He kicked Abdul's soccer ball into street," said Rachel in a rush. "And it got wrecked by a truck!"

Jordan was amazed that he could figure out what Rachel had just said. But it didn't help him know what to do to fix things. He pushed back his hair.

Mr. Allrite gazed at Abdul. "Is that why you're all upset?"

Abdul nodded. He spoke so quietly that Jordan could only lipread. "The ball was my birthday present."

Mr. Allrite pushed up his glasses. "It's time the principal learns about Max. I'll talk to you kids later."

Rachel faced Jordan. "Watching Max not

work out."

Jordan nodded, then shrugged. There was nothing they could do about it right now. *Go to class,* he gestured.

Some of the kids were painting scenery for the play. A large sailing ship—the Mayflower. Trees in a forest. A log cabin.

Jordan watched for a few minutes. His committee had nothing to work on this afternoon. He picked up a book and read a page. He put the book down. What would the principal do about Max?

The next morning, Jordan saw Abdul smiling. "What's up?" he asked his friend.

"I'm getting a new soccer ball today. Max has to buy it." Abdul laughed. "He won't bother you after school for a long time. He's busy working in his brother's store. Has to pay him back for the ball."

Jordan took a deep breath. Finally. A rest from that jerk.

In the afternoon, the actors walked around in their costumes. They practiced in front of the scenery.

Jordan saw Lisa hobble like an old Pilgrim. She signed to Abdul as Chief Massasoit. *Hello.*

He signed to her. *Hello.* Just like Pilgrims and Indians did long ago.

Uh, oh! Lisa's skirt dragged on the floor. She might trip! Jordan hurried to tell her.

Suddenly, Sabrina stepped in back of Lisa. Too close. Sabrina jumped on the hem. Rr-ip! The skirt tore and Lisa fell forward.

Jordan caught her. They looked into each other's faces.

She stood straight again. "I will ge-t even

with Sa-bri-na."

Jordan nodded. He had a feeling Max wasn't through causing trouble. And now Sabrina.

Chapter 12

But Sabrina was quiet the next day. So was Max. Maybe because of his visit to the principal's office.

Mr. Allrite spoke to the class. Sandy signed. *How would you like a party?*

Lisa glanced at her interpreter, then clapped. The others kids joined in.

You deserve some fun before rehearsals start. The teacher pushed up his glasses. *I have an hot-air popper. Who will bring the popcorn?*

Jordan thought that would be neat. "I will," he said.

"I will br-ing coo-kies," Lisa said.

"I can bake small cakes," said Rachel.

"Sounds delicious," said Mr. Allrite. Sandy signed his next words. *We can also use fruit, pretzels and napkins. Bring whatever you can.*

What day? Jordan signed.

The teacher ran a hand through his red hair. *How about in two days?*

Everyone clapped again.

After school, Jordan talked with Abdul.

"Wha-t you b-ring?"

"Some napkins," said Abdul. "Mom just bought a bunch."

Jordan nodded. "See you la-ter."

At home, he opened his Ninja Turtle bank. He shook out two wadded-up dollar bills. This was money he'd saved for something special. He'd use it for the party.

He walked past the fish market—to the variety store. He looked at the candy, pretzels and potato chips. He hoped the other kids would bring that stuff. He was bringing popcorn—something no one else needed to bring.

He picked up a sealed plastic bag of yellow kernels and paid for it. He whistled all the way home.

The day of the party, Jordan put the sealed bag inside a paper bag. He whistled all the way to school. He could hardly wait to hear the kernels pop.

Abdul brought a pile of white napkins.

Rachel brought six chocolate cupcakes. Blue candy sprinkles decorated the tops.

Other kids brought cupcakes too. Yellow with chocolate icing. White with pink peppermint icing.

Lisa brought orange pumpkin-shaped cookies.

Other kids brought cookies too. Chocolate chip, coconut, lemon. Some brought pretzels and potato chips.

A few brought plates and cups or napkins. They brought frozen orange juice and lemonade.

Mr. Allrite signed. *Jordan, Rachel. Please get two pitchers from the cafeteria. And long spoons.*

When they came back, he mixed the juice.

Jordan tried to open up the thick plastic bag of yellow kernels. He pulled the plastic. The bag wouldn't open. He tugged and tugged. It still wouldn't open.

He motioned to Abdul. They each held an end of the bag. Then they both pulled at the same time.

Pop! The bag opened and a bunch of kernels spilled out. Plap, plap, plap! They bounced all over the floor.

Sabrina slithered near. "Should have used scissors," she hissed. She turned away, nose in the air. And stepped on the kernels.

Whoops! Her right foot slid. Her left foot slid. She swung her arms to balance. But...thud! Down she fell.

Serves her right for tearing Lisa's skirt, thought Jordan.

"Help!" Sabrina yelled.

Max sprinted to her outstretched hand. Whoops! He slid on the kernels. And fell down—thud!

Jordan and Abdul grinned at each other and held the bag closed.

Rachel and Lisa laughed. But they got a broom and dustpan.

Mr. Allrite brought out the hot-air popper. "We better pop what's left," he said and signed.

Jordan poured some kernels into the popper. He rested his hand next to it. After a few minutes, he felt vibrations.

Fluffy white puffs popped inside the machine. Then they hopped out the funnel into a huge bowl. Fragrant steam swirled around the room.

Mr. Allrite unplugged the machine.

The kids grabbed paper plates and put handfuls of hot popcorn on them.

Max and Sabrina came toward the bowl. The kids pushed them away. Max and Sabrina came back. The kids pushed them away again. And again.

Finally, the horrible two got to the bowl. There was only one puff left for each of them!

Jordan chewed his crunchy popcorn. He grinned at Abdul again. Maybe Max and Sabrina would stop making trouble. Maybe....

On Monday, Mr. Allrite outlined the plans. "Serious rehearsals start now," he said and signed. "We'll work with props. We can use one classroom wall for scenery. Like a stage."

He smiled at them. "Each person can do something. We need some people who act, but don't speak lines. Who's interested?"

"I am!" shouted Max.

A couple of kids raised their hands.

"Okay," said and signed the teacher. He pointed at the two kids. "You can be Pilgrims." He pointed at Max. "You can be an Indian."

Jordan thought hard. Sometimes an audience clapped for the author of a play. He'd seen it on closed-captioned TV.

The play story was his idea. But other kids had written the lines. So he wasn't really the author. He rubbed his knuckles. What could he do to get applause?

Chapter 13

We need prompters," said Mr. Allrite. Sandy signed. *They will read lines to any actors that forget.*

"Choose me." "I want to." "Let me do that!" Several kids raised their hands.

Not me, thought Jordan. I'll be too busy directing props.

Hope we don't need that much help. Mr. Allrite laughed. *We only need one prompter for each side of the stage.* He pointed to a boy and a girl. *Your jobs. Now we also need people to take scenery on and off.*

Several other kids raised their hands.

Kris stood in front of Jordan. "Can I come back to your prop committee?" she asked.

He read her lips and nodded. With Max gone, she knows it'll be better, he thought.

Of course, Max wasn't really gone. Only off their prop committee. He was now an actor. Without lines to say because he didn't speak loud enough.

Jordan scratched his head. Max couldn't

yell on stage. Just everywhere else! Really weird.

Rehearsal started. Part of the classroom became a stage.

Act One. The scenery on the wall showed a ship. With old-fashioned split sails.

Jordan was in charge of all props. He directed and gestured. *Chairs on stage. Plymouth Rock on stage. Dolls for babies to Pilgrim women. Section of ship in place.*

Jordan walked down the steps to the floor in front of the stage. The audience would sit here and back farther.

He knew actors sat on the chairs. They sat between the wall scenery and the painted ship prop.

From the floor, all Jordan could see were Pilgrims sitting inside a ship. That's what the audience would see too. Good!

He went backstage again. He stood near the prop boxes.

Act Two. The scene with snowy trees, a log cabin and gray sky.

He directed and motioned. *Put dolls and Rock away. Fix chairs.* Jordan gave his helpers cardboard guns. He pointed, *give to Pilgrims.* He gave his helpers bows and arrows. *Give to Indians.* He opened the ladder in the stage wings.

Then he gave Rachel the bag of paper snow. Soapflakes were only for the performances. The actors said their lines. Jordan couldn't hear them. But he saw their lips moving. The act ended.

He motioned his helpers. *Put guns away. Bows and arrows away. Sweep up snow—put*

66

into the bag again. Fold chairs. Take them off stage.

Act Three. The scene showed a cabin and green trees. A yellow sun was painted in a blue sky. Jordan gave his helpers the digging tools and cardboard fish.

Max grabbed a fish. He waved it in front of Chief Massasoit's face. And in the faces of other actors.

They pretended to plant fish. But two Indians grabbed Max. They pushed him to plant his fish.

Hot anger filled Jordan. Max was spoiling their play!

At lunchtime, Jordan ate fish and chips with Abdul.

Max sprinted through the cafeteria.

"Jerk," said Abdul. "Trying to ruin our play."

Jordan nodded. "We mus-t sto-p him." He looked at his plate. Then he grinned at his friend and gestured. *Get some fish from the cafeteria cook.*

Abdul left. When he came back, he shook his head. "No fish, just frozen fish cakes. The cook wouldn't give me any. Too bad."

Jordan shrugged. He'd figure out a different way.

After school, he walked past his house to the fish store. He had some money left from buying the popcorn. So he bought a real fish.

Might be more fun if it was alive, he thought. But this would have to do.

The next morning, he put it inside his cubby at school. After lunch, he removed the package. He carried it into the classroom.

Rehearsal of Act Three. Prop helpers gave the fake fish to the Indians.

Jordan gestured, *I'll give one to Max.* He unwrapped the package. Yuk! This smelly piece of fish was perfect for Max. Jordan ran on stage. He gave the disgusting fish to disgusting Max. Then he ran off and watched.

His enemy clutched the raw fish. He tried to wave it around. But it slipped through his fingers—up into the air! Flip, flap, flop.

The smelly fish landed near the other actors. They frowned at Max. They held their fingers over their noses.

Max bit his lower lip.

Good. He's really embarrassed, thought Jordan. Maybe even crying?

Mr. Allrite's face reddened. He pointed to the floor and said something.

Max scooped up the fish. He ran to the hall and disappeared.

The class finished rehearsing Act Three. Jordan's helpers put away the cardboard fish. They changed the scenery and got ready to rehearse Act Four.

Jordan gave his helpers red, brown and gold leaves. They taped them on the trees. He gave them green apples to tie on the trees. The helpers set up a table and chairs.

Act Four started—Indians and Pilgrims, celebrating the first Thanksgiving. Jordan noticed one Pilgrim look at a prompter. The prompter's lips moved. The Pilgrim nodded. She turned to the stage and started talking again.

Abdul was wonderful as Chief Massasoit. He waved his bow at the Pilgrims. They quickly

68

grabbed guns and pointed them at the Indians.

Chief Massasoit shook his head. He pointed to the trees and beyond. Several Indians came onstage. They carried cardboard rabbits and turkeys.

The Pilgrims put down their guns.

Old lady Lisa hobbled forward to speak.

Jordan thought, Max isn't around. There won't be any trouble.

Then Sabrina entered, swishing her long skirt. She walked in front of Lisa and blocked her from sight.

Lisa stepped in front of Sabrina. "Thaannk...." She started to say her line.

Sabrina pushed her away. Then Sabrina walked back and forth, waving her arms. She pointed at the Indians. She pointed at other Pilgrims.

Jordan gulped. This wasn't right! The audience wouldn't see Lisa. They wouldn't hear her either. He watched everyone's lips.

The other actors stared. What was going on?

"Ah, rabbits and turkeys," Sabrina said. "Let us eat."

Jordan wanted to run on stage. Someone must stop Sabrina!

Chapter 14

Before he could make a move, Lisa jumped. Smack in front of the nasty girl, just like a kangaroo. "Coo-k foo-d!" she shouted.

Jordan burst out laughing. That wasn't Lisa's line.

"Some people try to spoil things," said a Pilgrim man.

"Stop, stop!" called Mr. Allrite. "Those aren't the right lines."

The two interpreters came to help with the teacher's words. *Practice more at home. We'll rehearse again tomorrow.*

The red light flashed for dismissal.

We must put away the props, thought Jordan. He motioned to his helpers. *Hurry, hurry, hurry!*

They rushed to get the props and put them into boxes. Jordan worried. There are so many props and so many boxes. What if there's a mixup?

The next afternoon, Mr. Allrite took the class to the gym. It was a huge room. A stage at one end had blue velvet curtains.

The teacher stood in front of Jordan. Sandy signed. *We'll rehearse here every day. We can keep our costumes behind curtains. Also the scenery and props.* He signed to Jordan. *Get the prop boxes.*

Jordan motioned to Kris, Rachel, and two boys. They hurried back to the classroom for the boxes. They carried them into the gym—to the stage.

"Let's start!" called out Mr. Allrite.

Jordan understood. He ran to the props.

Act One. He motioned to his helpers. *Put props on stage. Chairs, Plymouth Rock, dolls. Wait. Then hurry, hurry, hurry. Props off the stage and back into boxes.*

Act Two. *Props out of different boxes. Guns. Bows and arrows. Put the ladder up. Bag of paper snow. Rearrange chairs. Wait.... Now hurry. Faster, faster! Props off stage and into boxes. Sweep up snow. Chairs off.*

Act Three. *Hurry, hurry, hurry. Different props out of boxes. Digging tools and cardboard fish to actors. Wait...wait.... Quick! Props off stage, into boxes.*

Act Four. *Hurry. Faster, faster, faster. Two bags of leaves. Bag filled with apples. Ladder open. Tape leaves on the trees. Tie some apples on the trees. Put table and chairs on stage. Put rabbits and turkeys behind bushes.*

Take platters for fake food on stage. Careful! Don't break platters. Sweat dripped from Jordan's face and he wiped it off with his hands. Then he wiped his wet hands on his jeans. I better bring a towel tomorrow, he decided.

The play ended. *All props off stage and into boxes. Take the table off and fold the chairs. Done!*

Jordan took a deep breath. His outgoing breath whistled. He hadn't been nervous during rehearsal. But now! His stomach felt jumpy and his hands shook.

He checked the four prop boxes. Dolls, leaves, snow. Guns, arrows, apples. Bows, fish, tools. He scratched his head. Something was missing.

Where was Plymouth Rock? Jordan looked behind the ladder. It wasn't there. He looked in the dark stage corners. Not there. He crossed the stage. There it was—on the wrong side.

Jordan carried the Rock to the prop boxes. He hoped the other props were in their right places. There was no time to check now.

He hurried out of the gym. If any props were in the wrong boxes—he'd find out tomorrow.

Rehearsal was in full swing the next afternoon. Jordan motioned to the helpers for Act One. *Get chairs and Plymouth Rock. Put on stage.*

The helpers grabbed baby dolls from a box. There were only three. They needed four.

Jordan reached into the box. He felt something round. A doll's head? He pulled it up and looked. An apple. Wonder how that got in here. He put it into the bag with the other apples.

The actors were on the Mayflower ship, speaking. I'll find the fourth doll later, he thought.

The curtain closed and Jordan went into action. *Hurry, hurry, hurry.* He directed the

73

helpers. *Take props off stage. Put into box.* Uh, oh, he wondered. Why is the bag of snow here? He put it to the side.

Then Jordan prepared for Act Two. *Rachel, get the bag. Kris, get the ladder.* Jordan handed out this act's props. Bows, arrows and fish. Fish? We don't need fish yet, he thought.

We need the guns. Where are they? He searched the other boxes. He found guns next to the cardboard turkeys. "Here g-u-ns!" he called.

The helpers ran to get them. They rushed the guns to the Pilgrim men. They stood ready in front of the scenery painted with snowy trees.

Jordan watched from the wings. He watched the actors' lips. The curtain opened. Several Pilgrims huddled near a log cabin.

Sabrina looked at the sky. She said her line. "Oh, no! Here comes more snow!"

This was Rachel's cue to throw paper snow. She reached into the bag and threw—arrows!

Brown cardboard arrows fell, not white paper snow. Sabrina stamped her foot. "Rachel!" she shrieked. "You ruined my part."

All the other Pilgrims focused on Rachel and frowned.

"Stop that!" Mr. Allrite yelled at Sabrina. He walked to the ladder and looked up at Rachel. "What's going on?"

She stumbled down the steps with the bag. Tears spilled from her eyes. She picked up the arrows, put them into the bag. She handed it to Jordan without saying a word.

He found the bag with the fake snow. He handed it to Rachel.

She shook her head. *You do*, she signed.

So Jordan climbed the ladder. He tossed the snow at Sabrina and the other Pilgrims. Then he climbed down.

Some helpers were putting props away. Others were taking props out. Arrows fell on the floor. Fish fell on the floor. Helpers scooped them up. They gave the props to the actors.

"Wrong props!" The actors threw arrows at the helpers and laughed. "This time we need the fish!"

Jordan heard some sounds and read their lips. He dashed around picking up arrows. He put them in the Act Two box. Then he grabbed fish off the floor and gave them to the helpers.

He was out of breath. Sweat dripped down his back and soaked into his T-shirt. This was too much for him! *Kris, you can be in charge of set props,* he gestured. *Me and Rachel will give out hand props.*

Kris nodded. She brought the chairs off stage. She checked the bags of leaves and put them next to the ladder. She placed a roll of tape and one of string on the bottom step. "Where are the apples?" she asked.

Jordan searched the dark backstage corners. He found the bag—and Max!

Chapter 15

Max munched and slobbered eating two apples at the same time.

Jordan counted the apples in the bag. Only six left. There should have been ten. The missing four were probably in Max's stomach. Too angry to think, Jordan raced at his enemy. He pushed the apples out of his hands.

Max stumbled backward. He stuck out his tongue and ran away.

The curtain closed on Act Three. Helpers brought props off and dumped them into a box.

Jordan stopped them from reaching into the Act Four box. "No-o, no-o," he said, shaking his head at them. "I gi-ve." He gave out rabbits and turkeys. He gave out apples to tie on trees.

Rachel taped some leaves on the trees.

Kris climbed the ladder. She carried a bag filled with leaves to toss—as though they were falling from the trees.

The curtain opened on Act Four. While the kids acted, Jordan checked prop boxes. He signed to Kris and Rachel. *Come here.*

They sorted the props into the correct boxes. Arrows in the box with bows and guns. All the fish in another box.

No more mixups, Jordan thought. We're ready for dress rehearsal.

"Big day tomorrow," said Mr. Allrite. Sandy signed his next words. *The first graders will watch us.*

The next day, Jordan looked around the stage.Everybody was ready for dress rehearsal. His foot kicked a half-eaten apple. What was Max up to?

The curtain opened smoothly. The actors knew their lines. No mixups in Act One. The first graders clapped and clapped.

Jordan and his committee prepared for Act Two. Kris carried the bag of snow. She was ready to climb the ladder.

Max sprinted past. He grabbed the bag out of her arms. He laughed and dashed out of the gym.

Kris ran to Jordan. "What should I do?" she cried.

Jordan looked for more paper. He could tear it for snow. But the curtain was opening on the next act. It was too late.

Sabrina looked up at the gray sky. She spoke her first line. "Oh, no! Here comes more snow." Nothing fell. "More snow," she said louder.

Jordan climbed the ladder. He shook his head at her. He waved his arms, *no*.

Sabrina got the message. "No more snow!" she shouted. "Just icy cold."

When the curtain closed, Sabrina ran to Jordan. "What happened?" she shrieked.

"M-ax t-ook s-now," he said. Then he gestured, *He ran away with the bag.*

Sabrina stamped her foot. "He's not my friend any more!"

Jordan shrugged. What did Sabrina's words really mean? Was she on their side now? He prepared for Act Three.

Max sprinted onto the stage wearing his Indian costume. He darted around, touching the trees.

Weird jerk, thought Jordan.

The curtain opened. From the wings, Jordan saw the actors look surprised. Then angry. Why? He knew this wasn't part of the story.

A few seconds later, the play continued. Max planted cardboard fish with other Indians. The Pilgrims watched. Finally, the curtain closed.

Abdul stood in front of Jordan. "Did you hear laughing?"

"No," said Jordan. "Saw some-thi-ng wro-ng. Not und-ersta-nd. Wh-at ha-ppen-ed?

There was snow on the trees," said Abdul. "In summer! All the little kids laughed. It almost spoiled the play. Who did it?"

Jordan frowned. So that's what Max had been up to when he touched trees! He'd taped on snow. "I th-ink Max di-d it," said Jordan.

"He should be tied up," said Abdul.

Jordan nodded. *Good idea*, he signed. He slapped hands with Abdul. "We tie h-im be-fore rea-l play sta-rt-s."

Abdul walked away. Jordan prepared the Act Four props.

Kris, Rachel and the helpers took snow off

the trees. They put the paper scraps into a bag. They attached leaves and apples to the trees.

Kris climbed the ladder. Rachel handed her the bag of dry leaves.

Jordan watched as the curtain opened. Chief Massasoit, who was really Abdul, came on stage. He waved his bow and arrow.

Some Pilgrims pointed guns at some Indians. Other Indians carried rabbits and turkeys onto the stage.

Old Pilgrim lady, really Lisa, hobbled toward them.

Sabrina swished on stage. Her hair was covered by a stiff bonnet.

Jordan held his breath. Sabrina might be angry at Max. But would that keep her from spoiling Lisa's part again?

Sabrina stopped next to the old lady and curtsied.

The old lady smiled. She pointed to the Indians carrying turkeys and rabbits. "Thankyu!" she said.

"Yes, thank you, too," Sabrina said. "Let's cook a feast."

Jordan's breath whistled out of his mouth. He put his hand over it. He smiled. Sabrina really cared about the play.

Now there was only one enemy—Max. And he'd be tied up tomorrow. Only...where should they tie him?

Jordan looked at the dark corners. Only one had a post. No one would see Max tied up there. It was a good place. And then that obnoxious boy couldn't spoil the class play.

Satisfied, Jordan watched the final curtain close. The story was my idea, he thought. I wish I could be on stage somehow.

Then the audience would see him. They would know he was special. Deaf special—<u>and</u> acting special. Jordan wanted applause. He wanted to see kids clapping just for him.

Could he still learn a part? Not enough time, he thought sadly. And I can't hear enough. Or speak enough words. People wouldn't understand what I said.

Hurry, hurry, hurry! he thought. Think of a way to be on stage. The performance is tomorrow. I need to tell Mr. Allrite before it's too late. Jordan blew air through his teeth.

"Nice whistling!" exclaimed Kris.

He stopped in surprise. Whistle? Sure. He rushed to his teacher with an idea.

Mr. Allrite signed, *That should work okay. The audience will like it.*

All the way home, Jordan whistled. He felt happy inside. Especially later, when he found a long rope for tying Max. He put it into his pocket. He'd use the rope tomorrow—before the play started.

Chapter 16

But what if the jerk yelled? Someone would come and untie him. He better have a gag for Max. What should he use?

Jordan looked in his mother's linen closet. He took out a small washcloth. *I can put this in his mouth. It will stop him from yelling, without hurting him. And he'll still be able to breathe.*

He stuffed the washcloth into his pocket. Now he had a rope in one pocket and a gag in the other. He was all set. He'd wear these same jeans again tomorrow.

Performance day arrived. The actors paced back and forth near the closed curtains. Kids placed the scenery for Act One. The Mayflower was set up.

Jordan rubbed the knuckles of his hand. He stood by the prop boxes and directed helpers. *Put chairs and Rock on stage.* He grinned at Abdul wearing the biggest feather headress. He waved to Lisa in her perfect Pilgrim skirt. Then he motioned to Rachel.

Give the dolls to Pilgrim women.

Sabrina came up to Lisa and Abdul. She said something and they laughed.

Abdul came to tell Jordan. "Sabrina said 'Break a leg!' It's what theater people say before a performance. Means good luck."

Jordan laughed. "O-kay! Brea-k leg." He turned back to the prop boxes.

Max stood there.

He can't spoil our play, thought Jordan. His fingers touched the rope in his pocket. There was no time to waste!

They must tie Max up right now, before the play started. Jordan motioned, *come here*, to Abdul.

His friend nodded and they walked to the post in the dark corner.

Jordan's stomach cramped and his mouth went dry. "Ma-axx," he called. "C-ome he-re. We wa-nt to show you so-methin-g."

His enemy looked up, then sprinted over. "What're you guys doing?"

"This!" exclaimed Abdul. He pulled Max against the post.

Jordan whipped out the rope. Whoosh! He wrapped it around the post and Max—three times. Around his arms. Around his middle. Around his ankles.

Max opened his mouth to yell.

Jordan stuck the washcloth over his mouth.

Abdul wrapped tape over it and around Max's head. There! Jordan grinned at Abdul.

I feel like a rodeo cowboy, he thought. Max is the roped calf! He wiped his hands on his jeans and walked to the prop boxes.

84

Abdul joined the other Indians as the curtain opened.

Mr. Allrite stood in the wings. Sandy stood on one side of the stage. Lisa's interpreter stood on the other side. The two of them interpreted for the deaf kids sitting in the front row.

Act One. The actors look like real Pilgrims, Jordan thought. They came to a strange place. They had hard times. Just like me, coming to this school. No deaf friends.

Jordan knew the action by heart. The Pilgrims landing at Plymouth Rock. Met by the Indians who lived there. Pilgrims afraid of Indians. Indians afraid of Pilgrims.

Then Act Two—the terrible winter. Cold and icy. Snow falling. Pilgrims sick and dying. That's how he had felt when this class started.

In Act Three—Indians show Pilgrims how to plant and use fish for fertilizer. They start trusting each other.

Jordan remembered starting to trust Rachel, Lisa and Abdul. Now they were his friends. And Kris was too.

He looked back to where they'd tied Max. Still there, squirming like a worm on a fishhook! And nobody missed him!

Jordan smiled. He felt thankful like the Pilgrims. He turned toward the stage again.

The curtain opened on Act Four. Hey, he remembered. I have a part to do! Jordan dashed past Max—into the dressing room. He pulled on a Pilgrim jacket and trousers. He grabbed a tall hat and rushed out.

At the stage, Jordan took a deep breath. He was ready for his part that would end the play. He put on the Pilgrim hat and walked forward.

He whistled while crossing the stage to Chief Massasoit. Jordan held up his hand. "Th-ank-s a l-o-t," he said to the Chief, really his friend Abdul.

Abdul grinned—and signed, *okay*. Then the two friends bowed to each other.

Everyone clapped and clapped. The deaf kids, the other kids. His mother, father and Mr. Allrite. His other friends on stage. Especially Rachel and Lisa.

Jordan smiled as he bowed again. He was deaf. He used sign language and spoke a few words. The kids in this school could understand him. He could understand them.

Warmth flowed from his head to his toes. It felt great to be exactly who he was.

The End